This Ladybird book

belongs to

N un

Published by Ladybird Books Ltd
80 Strand London WC2R 0RL
A Penguin Company

10 9

Printed in Italy

Goodnight
Little Bunny

by Ronne Randall
illustrated by Sophie Harding

Ladybird

Little Bunny had been playing
in the wood all the long afternoon.
But now the sun was sinking
behind the trees. Old Owl looked
down at Little Bunny and said,

"Tu-whit, tu-whoo,
too late for you!"

Little Bunny looked up. "It's not
too late!" he said. "I'm going to
find someone to play with!"

And off he went...

skippety skip, hoppety hop...

...straight to Little Mouse's house.

But Little Mouse and his baby brothers and sisters were all ready for bed!

"You need your sleep, too, Little Bunny," said Mrs Mouse.

"Run home, Little Bunny, hurry along! Snug in your bed is where you belong!"

"Only babies go to bed!" said Little Bunny. "I'll roll acorns instead!"

And off he went...

skippety skip, hoppety hop...

He found a nice round, smooth acorn and rolled it and flicked it and kicked it...

...straight into Hedgehog's den!

"I was fast asleep!" grumbled Hedgehog. "And you should be asleep, too, Little Bunny!

"Run home, Little Bunny,
hurry along!
Snug in your bed
is where you belong!"

"Bed is boring!" said Little Bunny. "I'll chase butterflies instead!"

And off he went...

skippety skip, hoppety hop...

But the butterflies had all folded their wings and gone to sleep.

Suddenly a lacy-winged moth flitter-fluttered past Little Bunny, whispering,

"Run home, Little Bunny,
hurry along!
Snug in your bed
is where you belong!"

"No it isn't!" Little Bunny whispered back. "I'll race with my shadow instead!"

But Little Bunny couldn't catch
his shadow in the soft,
silvery moonlight.

And off he went...

skippety skip, hoppety hop...

...right up to his own front door, where Mother Bunny was waiting for him with a hug and a cuddle saying,

"You're home, Little Bunny,
now come along.
Your snug little bed
is where you belong!"

"Perhaps you are right," said a tired Little Bunny...

...And with that Little Bunny climbed into his bed and snuggled down with a warm, cosy hug!

Goodnight, Little Bunny!